SNOW
BEAR

For Daniel and Nicholas

This edition produced for
The Book People Ltd,
Hall Wood Avenue, Haydock,
St Helen's, WA11 9UL.

ISBN 1-85613-671-X

Manufactured in China.

SNOW BEAR

Illustrated by Piers Harper

Little Snow Bear had been snuggled up with his mother all winter inside their cosy den, but today the sun was shining and he was longing to go outside.

"It's time for you to meet the world, my little one," said his mother.

Little Snow Bear tumbled outside, slipping and sliding in the soft powdery snow. It was so much fun he did it again and again! "Now you can go and explore," said his mother, "but stay by the water's edge where I can see you. I don't want you getting lost."

Little Snow Bear didn't know what lost was. He didn't even know what water was. But if both were as much fun as snow, he couldn't wait to find out.

He rushed down to the water. It was blue and shimmery, and it went right out to the edge of the world. It was the most beautiful thing he had ever seen.

And there was something else, too. Something was dancing
in the water, making it ripple and splash.

"Hello," said a little seal. "I've been waiting for you to come out of your den. Do you want to play?"
The water looked so exciting that Little Snow Bear jumped right in – splash! Exploring was such fun.

Little Snow Bear had a lovely time playing splashing games with his new friend, but as the sun went down, he remembered what his mother had said. He looked around, but he couldn't see his mother anywhere. He pulled himself out of the water, shook himself dry, and set off to find her.

Little Snow Bear padded across the ice, but he soon found himself in a dark forest. He was just starting to feel a little worried when he heard a friendly voice.

"Hello there," said a reindeer. "What are you doing here all alone?"

"I'm exploring," said Little Snow Bear, "but now I need to find my mother."

"Come with me," said the reindeer kindly.
I'll show you the way out of the forest."

The kind reindeer showed him back to the icy world where
Little Snow Bear was sure his mother would be waiting . . .
but she wasn't there! Suddenly exploring wasn't so much fun.
His tummy rumbled, he felt hungry, and he wanted his mother.
Then Little Snow Bear smelled something familiar. FISH!

"Hello," said a girl. "What are you doing out here all alone?"

"I'm exploring," Little Snow Bear said gloomily. "I was having fun, but now I'm hungry and tired, and I want my mother."

"Little Snow Bear, I think you're lost," said the girl.

"But this is no fun," whimpered Little Snow Bear.

"No," said the girl. "Getting lost is no fun at all. But don't worry, I know where to find your mother."

So, after a delicious fish meal, Little Snow Bear
climbed into the girl's sledge.
"Come on," she said to her dogs. "Let's take this
Little Snow Bear home to his mother."
And off they sped across the snow.

Little Snow Bear ran to his mother.
"Where have you been?" she said. "I've been
so worried about you."
"I'm sorry, I got lost," said Little Snow Bear.

"I've been exploring the world,"
he explained. "I found out that there
are lots of fun things to do, and lots
of exciting places . . .

"... but being home with you
is the very best place of all."